Dedication

לע"נ
ר' אברהם בן ר' דוד הכהן ע"ה
ר' משה בן ר' חיים ברוך ע"ה
מרת פעסיל לפשא בת ר' יקותיאל יהודה ע"ה
מרת ראכל מיניא בת ר' אברהם שלמה הכהן ע"ה

This book would not have been possible without the help I received on many fronts. I have tremendous *hakaros hatov* to:

- The *Ribbono Shel Olam* for giving me the *koach* and talent to help people overcome their academic and social challenges.
- My dear parents ר' אברהם בן ר' דוד הכהן ע"ה, and Mommy, מרת שיינדל ראטה עמו"ש. As parents, they ingrained *mentchlichkeit* in their children and were models of love and inner strength.
- My dear husband, Chaim Boruch יחי', for his constant help, support, and encouragement.
- My wonderful, precious *kinderlach* and *ainikel* יחיו: Elimelech and Chavi, Yehuda, Sarala, Moishe, Sruli, Aryeh and little Mindy.
- My talented and dedicated daughter Sarala תחי', who stayed up nights helping me with every detail in this book.
- My valued siblings יחיו: Duvid, Chaytchie, and Ruchji who are always there for me, encouraging me to keep writing and helping people.
- My dear friend Raizel תחי', a remarkable woman who always encourages me to pursue my dreams.
- My cherished friend Ruchie תחי', who added valuable insights and enthusiastically gave me the courage to publish this book.
- My dear friend Yael תחי', who used her talents to critically read the early versions of the manuscript.
- My special friends יחיו: Reb Zev, Rebitzen Rochel, Rebitzen Rifka, Renee, Esther, Estie, Roz, Rifkie, Anita and Aleeza for all their inspiration.
- Dena at Dynagrafik and her staff for the skillful design, typesetting, and graphics of this book and with special thanks to Yoel Judowitz for his marvelous illustrations.
- Feldheim Publishers for their valuable advice and expertise.

Dear Readers:

Throughout the more than thirty years that I have been in education, I have noticed the intense problem of bullying in our schools. While I have worked individually with dozens of children to help them overcome bullies and written multiple articles concerning this topic, I felt that there needed to be a way to tackle this issue and reach a larger audience. For this reason, I decided to write a children's book that can be read both in the classroom and at home. As they enjoy the colorful pictures, the children will discover important tools and resources to combat bullies. In addition, the back section of the book contains tips for parents and schools in order to minimize and prevent bullying in the classroom.

How to Use this Book:

When reading this book, ask the children questions that allow them to think critically about the situation, such as:

- What is a bully?
- Why was Yossi being mean to Pinny?
- How come none of the other boys stopped Yossi?
- Who does Pinny turn to for help?
- What makes Yossi stop bullying Pinny?

Some questions that can help children work through their own problems with bullies are:

- Did someone ever treat you the way Yossi treated Pinny?
- What can you do if you see someone being bullied?
- Have you ever bullied someone else? Why?
- Is there something a teacher can do to prevent bullying in the classroom?

Research shows that if we make children aware of bullying patterns, we can take steps towards prevention. My hope is that this book is one more step in the right direction. I welcome your questions and comments.

Sincerely,
Rifka Schonfeld
(718) 382 - 5437

Author: Rifka Schonfeld

ISBN 978-1-58330-334-4

Distributed by Feldheim
POB 43163 / Jerusalem, Israel
208 Airport Executive Park, Nanuet, NY 10954
www.feldheim.com
Printed in Israel

My Friend the Bully

That's me, Pinny, with the red hair. Later you'll meet Yossi. There are twenty-five boys in my class, but Yossi and I have been in the same class since we were three years old. Most people think we are friends, but I know the truth. Sometimes Yossi is nice to me, but he's not my friend.

Since the beginning of the year, Yossi has been making me feel sad. One time when we were in the yard during recess, I saw Yossi playing handball with Moshe. I called out loudly, “Yossi can I play with you?”

And Moshe turned around, but Yossi didn't even look in my direction. I asked one more time, but Yossi just pretended he didn't hear me, while Moshe looked quietly at the ground. After a minute, I left to join the boys playing dodgeball on the other side of the yard.

Later that day, on the school bus when Yossi was by himself, I worked up the courage to ask him, “Why didn’t you answer me when you were playing handball?”

All Yossi did was shrug his shoulders and say, “It was a very important game.” I tried to shrug my shoulders too and pretend I didn’t care, but I still didn’t understand why he would ignore me like that.

Recently, things have been only getting worse. One day, Reuven and I were changing into our baseball uniforms after school, waiting for my mother to take us to the ball field. Yossi came up to me and dropped a note in my hand.

It said, "*If you talk to Reuven, I won't be your friend anymore.*"

When I finished reading the note, my face got all red and I stared at Yossi, but he just smiled and walked out of the building.

From that day on, whenever Yossi saw me talking to Reuven, he would wag his finger at me.

"What does Yossi have against Reuven?" I wondered, "Why can't we be friends?" But, soon, instead of shaking his finger at me, if Yossi noticed that I was talking to Reuven, he would purposely trip me as I walked down the aisle in the classroom. Rebbi wouldn't know why I fell, so Yossi would help me up to show him what good *midos* he had.

Then Rebbi would say, “Everybody should learn from Yossi to help people when they fall.” Yossi would smile and wink in my direction.

Things got so bad with my "friend" Yossi that I started telling my mother that I had a stomachache and didn't feel well enough to go to class. "Do you have a fever, Pinny?" my mother asked worriedly.

"I don't think so," I answered, "but I really feel sick."

My mother looked at my face and said, "You do look sick – you're right. Maybe you should stay home today."

But after two days of that, I knew I couldn't stay home forever, so I headed back to school.

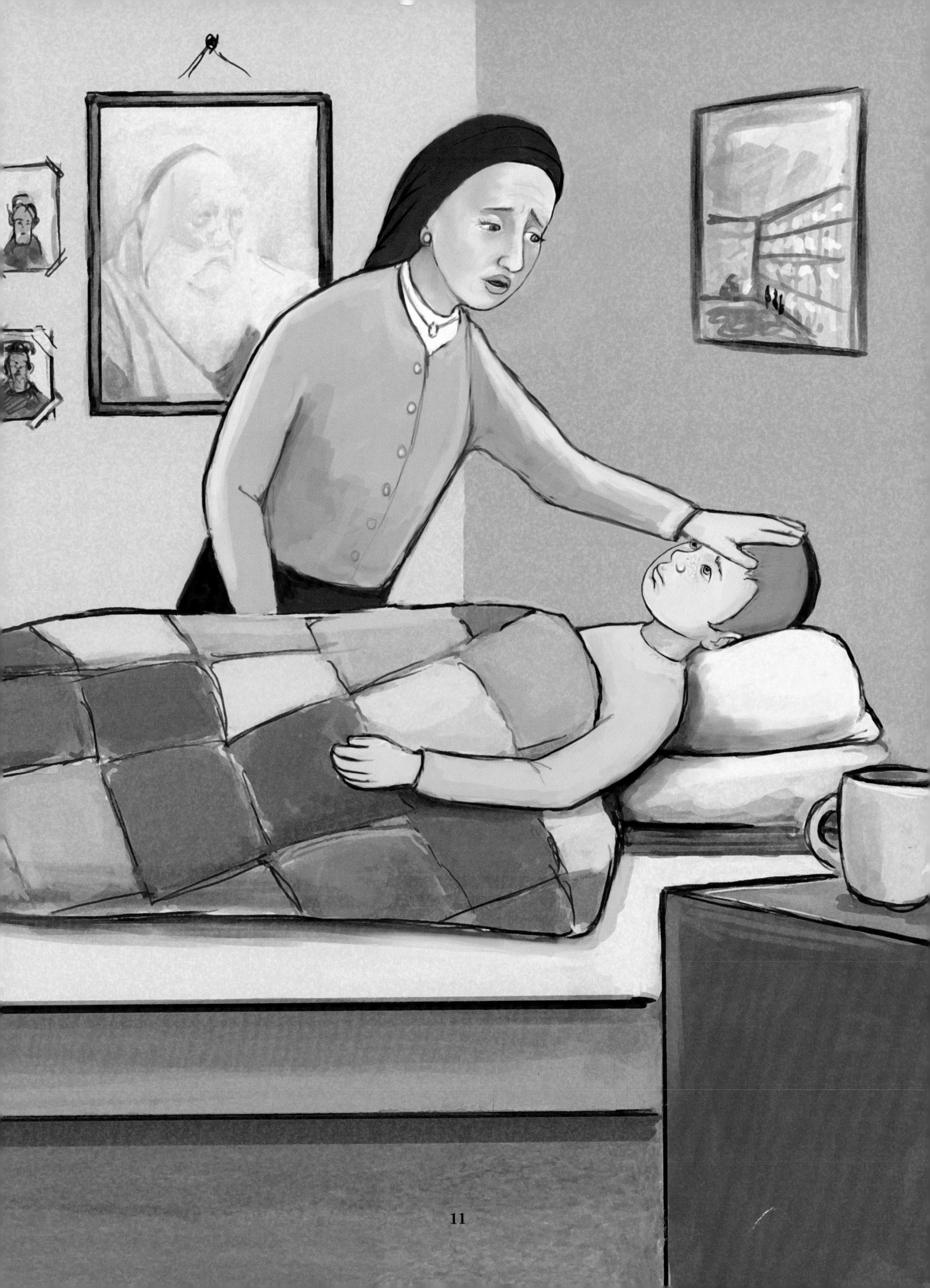

Just last week in the lunchroom when I walked up to the table in the cafeteria, Yossi pointed to my tuna fish sandwich and screamed, "That stinks! I can't believe you can eat that!" He started laughing so loudly that the rest of the boys at the table joined in.

I could tell that they didn't really think it was so funny, especially because sometimes they bring their own tuna fish sandwiches to school, but they laughed anyway.

After a few minutes, I said that my stomach hurt and I snuck out to the bathroom for the rest of lunch. No one seemed to notice that I left the table – they just kept on talking.

When I got home from school, I started yelling at my mother, "Why do you have to send me tuna fish sandwiches! They smell. Why can't you just send me something normal for lunch?" My mother stared at me and watched the tears fill my eyes.

"Pinny, you always eat tuna fish. Why don't you want it anymore?" she asked me. "I HATE TUNA FISH!" I yelled, as I raced up the stairs to my room.

After a few minutes, my mother came into my room and sat next to my bed. She noticed that my pillow was wet from my tears. "Pinny, this cannot be about tuna fish. What is going on?" she said as she rubbed my back. I looked at her and knew she wanted to help, so I started from the beginning with Yossi in the yard and ended with the tuna fish incident at lunch that day.

When I was done talking, my mother grabbed a tissue and wiped my eyes. She hasn't done that since I was younger, but I guess she could tell that I was feeling really sad. Then she said, "I am glad that you told me about this. It doesn't sound like Yossi is your friend. And, you don't deserve to be treated this way. Together, we are going to figure out a way to make all this stop."

After dinner with my family, Totty, Mommy, and I sat down in the living room. I knew this was serious because both my parents were taking time out of their busy schedules to talk to me about Yossi. First, I told my father everything I had told my mother earlier. Then, my parents took turns giving me advice.

My mother said, "Pinny, I know it might not seem that way, but bullies are mean to other people because they feel badly about themselves. Yossi makes fun of you in order to make himself feel better." I couldn't believe my mother was saying that, but when I thought about it, it made sense. Yossi would try to hurt me so other people wouldn't pick on him.

Then, my father told me how he thought I should respond to Yossi, "First, you have to show Yossi that you are unafraid and strong. Walk tall and with confidence. Then, if he says something mean to you in front of other people, ask him, 'Does it make you feel good to make me feel bad?' Or, 'Are you having a bad day? Is that why you are taking it out on me?'"

I practiced what I would say a few times with my father. Totty would say something mean and then I would react. At first, I would get hot and angry, even though I knew it was only pretend. But, after a few tries, I was able to be calm enough to realize that the insults had nothing to do with me. My father even gave me a special badge that he made for me that said, "You can, if you think you can." He called it my badge of courage to remind me of the inner strength I have.

I went to sleep that night worried about the next day, but a little less scared now that I didn't feel so alone. At least now my parents knew about Yossi. Also, at least I was a little prepared.

The next day, in the lunchroom, when I sat down at the table, Yossi turned to me and snorted loudly, "Pinny, no tuna fish today? What stinky food did you bring instead?"

At first I got all hot and just wanted to run away. But then, I felt my badge of courage, "You can, if you think you can." So, I took a deep breath, straightened my shoulders and said, "Yossi, how come you are so mean to me? Does it make you feel good to be mean?" Yossi turned bright red, everyone at the table stopped chewing, and I simply walked away.

Later that day, at recess, Moshe and Reuven turned to me and asked, "Want to play handball?" "Of course," I answered. When Yossi asked to join, I said, "Sure," but didn't try to chat with him after the game, like I normally would have. Instead, I walked to class with Reuven.

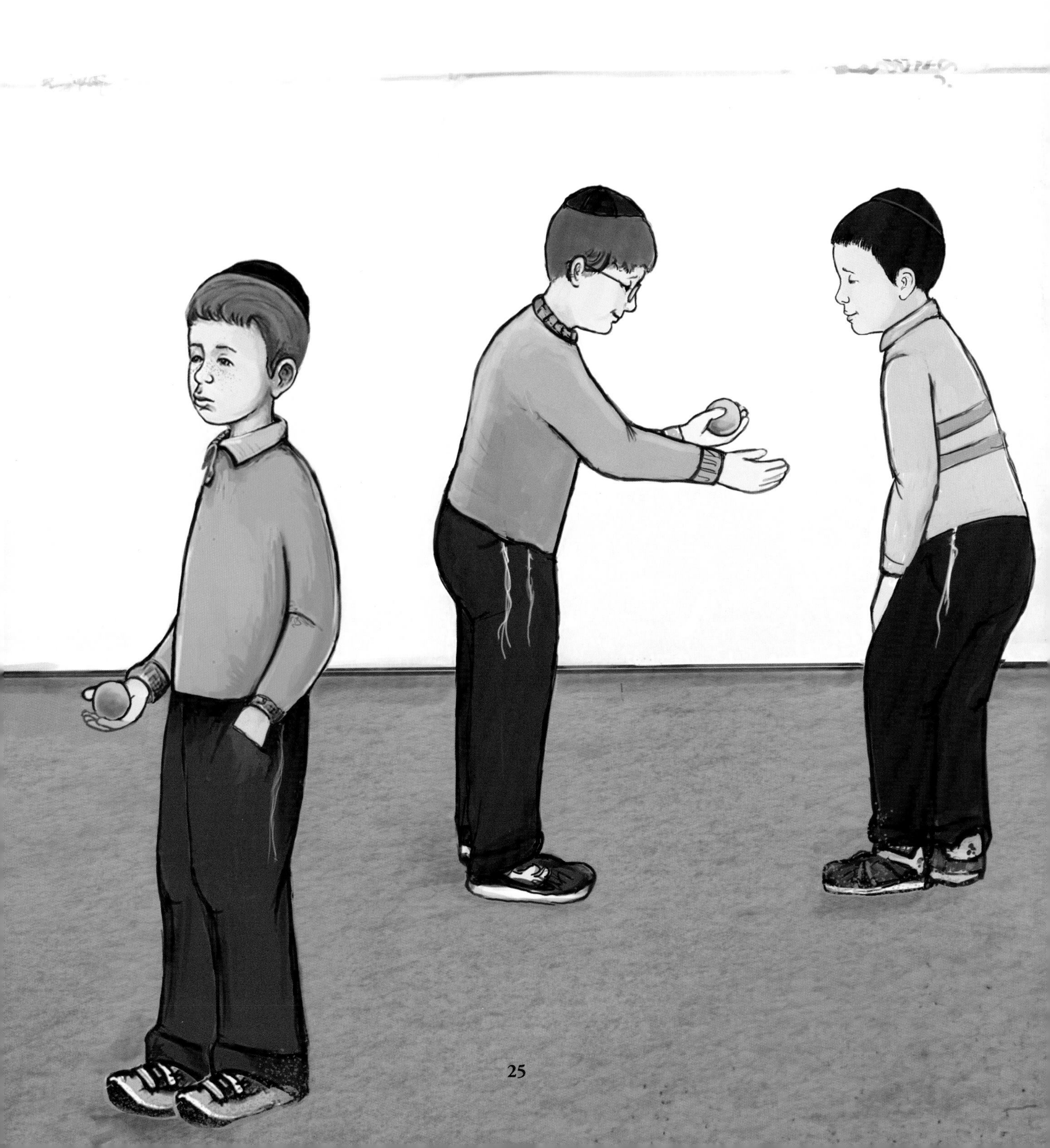

Lately things have been great at school. I learned one thing. Don't keep secrets! My parents wound up speaking with my Rebbi and the Menahel. Then, the school decided to have an assembly to speak to all of the students about bullying. My grades are even improving because I'm not worrying about Yossi anymore.

Deep down inside, I forgive him and even feel sorry for him, but it will be a while before I can fully trust him.

Best of all, my "stomachaches" are all gone!

Facts about Bullying

- According to the Journal of the American Medical Association, over 30% of children are estimated to be involved in bullying, either as a bully or a target of bullying.
- Each year, 160,000 students miss at least one day of school because they fear dealing with a bully.
- If bullying continues for a prolonged time, it can affect children's self esteem and self-worth, leading them to become withdrawn, depressed, anxious, and insecure.
- Those who act as bullies seem to maintain these characteristics into adulthood (if not properly intervened), negatively influencing their ability to develop mature adult relationships.
- When there is a school-wide commitment to end bullying, it can be reduced by up to 50%.

Tips for parents

Possible Warning Signs that Your Child is Being Bullied

- Returns home from school with torn, damaged, or missing clothing
- Seems afraid of going to school
- Suddenly begins to do poorly in school
- Complains frequently of headaches, stomachaches, or other illnesses.
- Has trouble sleeping or frequent bad dreams
- Appears anxious or suffers from low self-esteem

How to Stop the Bullying Cycle

- Talk to your child. Tell your child that you are concerned about them and that you would like to help them. You can ask direct questions such as, "Are there any kids at school who treat you meanly?"

Or indirect questions such as, "Are there any kids at school who you really don't like? Why?" Broaching the topic is the first step towards prevention.

- Listen to your child. Allow your child to share his fears and frustrations.
- Keep your emotions in check. Of course, you need to empathize with your child, but if you become overly emotional, your child will hesitate before talking to you about it again. Stay calm so that you can act as a supportive figure in your child's life.
- Talk to the staff at your child's school. Set up an appointment and explain that you are concerned. Ask questions about what you can do and what measures the school can take to prevent bullying. If you are not comfortable talking to your child's teacher, make an appointment with a principal or the school's guidance counselor.
- Teach your child to walk with confidence. If your child appears confident and walks away from the situation, he is signaling to the bully that the bully cannot hurt him.
- Encourage other friendships. Promote true friendships by telling your child to invite other children for play dates or study dates.

Tips for Schools and Teachers

The Center for the Study and Prevention of Violence recommends a school-wide approach to eliminating bullies:

- raising awareness about bullying through school programming
- increasing teacher and parent involvement and supervision
- forming clear rules and strong social norms against bullying
- providing support and protection for all students

This approach involves teachers, principals, students, and everyone associated with the school, including janitors, cafeteria workers, and crossing guards. These adults become aware of the extent of bullying at the school, and they involve themselves in changing the situation, rather than looking the other way. Students pledge not to bully other students, and to help students who are bullied.

You can,
if
you think
you can!